# Killer Kidz

A Zombie Novel

Brooke Luther

Killer Kidz Copyright © 2026 Brooke Luther

All rights reserved.

ISBN:979-8-90329-703-0

# Contents

# Dedication

For my kids. If you work hard you can do or be anything you want to. Make your dreams come true.

For my amazing, loving and supportive husband, Austin. Thank you for all of your support and love during this process.

I love you all more than a zombie loves brains.

# The Institute

## Rachel

## 2021

# Prologue

The party. It had to be the party. Rachel's head swarms with ideas of the last time she felt like herself. The last time she felt healthy. The last time she felt...normal.

She wasn't supposed to be there. She wasn't allowed to go. Her parents didn't think it would be a good idea. More than half of her class was out sick with this flu and who knows who else could be contagious. Her parents thought it was too big of a risk. But all of her friends were going: Zoe, Elijah, and Taylor. It's not like they were cliff jumping risking their lives. It was just a party. If her parents knew that she went though, she would be risking her life.

As Rachel paces back and forth in her room at The Institute, another thought crosses her mind. Not that her room wasn't really a room, it was more of a decontamination cube. Stark white walls and one way glass lining one side. A bed is in one corner and a toilet seat in the other. There were no windows. The only thing that told her it was time for bed was when they turned the lights off. The lights came on again in the morning.

She was thinking about telling her parents the truth. How she really got sick. She might not get the chance to if she doesn't do it soon. This virus, this disease has killed everyone who's infected with it except the kids who are going crazy. At least that's what the doctors are saying.

Rachel wonders if she's going to die or go crazy too.

The bite mark on her shoulder is only getting worse. It's red and swollen like a bruise and the puss coming out from it makes her smell worse than dog shit.

She imagines the doctors just staring at her through the one way glass. Watching her. Waiting for her to turn or die.

Rachel's parents rushed her here after she developed a fever. That's what the news told them to do. She woke up late in the afternoon looking like a rabid animal. She had a killer headache and she couldn't stop vomiting. She thought maybe someone had spiked her drink. But again, she couldn't exactly tell her parents that since she wasn't supposed to be out.

She didn't think the bite mark was a big deal at first. Just some guy getting a little frisky at the party after too many drinks. But it hurts like hell now. She covered it up with a sweater to hide the evidence when she was home.

The doctors say that bites are what transmits the disease, and it's getting harder and harder for Rachel to keep it a secret. Her fever hasn't come down since she's been here and her body rejects anything she tries to eat.

The kids at school started making jokes about The Institute. Saying that the kids that go in don't ever come out.

Later that night Rachel ends up convulsing on the cold floor of her decontamination cube. Choking on her own bile and salvia. Blood and snot start to run down her face.

Maybe the kids at school were right. Maybe she won't come out of here alive.

# Rachel

## 2020

# Chapter 1

ugust 20, 2020 was the first day of Rachel's senior year of high school. It was also her 17th birthday. She wakes up to her alarm on her phone, and with a drowsy hand she slips out of her blankets and hits the snooze button. She retreats back into her cocoon and falls back asleep. Ten minutes later her alarm goes off again.

This time she actually emerges from her warm cocoon and is greeted by the sun coming up over the mountain range. She gets dressed, brushes her teeth, combs her long brown hair, then makes her way downstairs.

She enters the kitchen of their classic suburban home and notices a note on the counter surrounded by balloons. The note has "Happy birthday, sweety. Love, Mom and Dad" written on it in her mother's handwriting. She smiles at it then grabs her school bag filled with supplies and heads out of the door.

She inhales the fresh mountain morning air and soaks in what might be the last warm day in Colorado. She walks two houses down and waits for her friend. They are going to take the bus together. Her friend stumbles out of her house.  Her long black hair is in a high pony on top of her head and her pale skin shines bright against her black clothes.

"Good morning, sunshine!" Rachel calls out to her friend.

All she gets back in return is a low grunt. Clearly her friend isn't a morning person. Her friend starts digging around in the front pocket of her bag and brings out a chocolate bar.

"Here, happy birthday." Her friend gives her a half smile which either matches her personality or is another sign that she still isn't awake.

Rachel's eyes light up with glee. "Thank you, Zoe!" You remembered!" She wasn't really surprised that her best friend since kindergarten remembered her birthday, but that she remembered her favorite chocolate bar.

"The breakfast of champions." Zoe jokes as she grabs a Starbucks can next out from her bag.

The girls giggle as they make their way to the bus stop and enjoy their treats while they wait for the bus to arrive.

*****

Rachel's first day of school went great. She had AP English with Zoe, calculus, Art 4, then government. She was never really good at history so she was glad she saw her friend Taylor when she walked into the room. He's a huge history nerd.

When she arrived home she was welcomed by her mother with a warm hug and a kiss.

"Happy birthday, sweetheart! How was your first day?" Rachel's mom always liked hearing about her day, even when she was small that was the first question she would ask.

"It was fine." Rachel's reply was a typical response for that question. It was known world wide by all parents of teenagers. "I had English with Zoe and government with Taylor."

"Oh that's great, sweety! I'm glad you got to see your friends on your birthday! Dad will be home soon and then we'll celebrate with your birthday dinner and cake."

"Sounds great!" Rachel was excited for her birthday dinner. She may not look like it, but she LOVES to eat. Her favorite meal is a nice rare steak with a mountain of potatoes on the side. They saved those kinds of meals for special occasions since the meat was so expensive. And she can't wait for her favorite cake. Triple layered chocolate with chocolate fudge on top. The kind of cake that makes your teeth ache after eating it.

Rachel goes up to her room and gets cleaned up before her dad gets home. She puts on an old t-shirt and a pair of sweatpants; good pants for eating steak and triple chocolate cake. About twenty minutes later Dad comes home.

Dinner is served thanks to Mom and they all sit at the table to enjoy the birthday meal.

"How was your day, honey?" Dad asks Rachel over a mouthful of potatoes.

Rachel finishes chewing on a piece of her rare steak. "It was fine. I had English with Zoe today."

"That's your friend with the black hair and the thing in her nose right?"

Rachel rolls her eyes. "Yeah, Dad it's called a nose ring."

Mom gives Dad a light tap on his shoulder. Persuading him from making any more fun of his daughter's friends. The rest of the dinner is uneventful and they finish in peace. Mom grabs the cake from the fridge and lights a number 17 candle. Mom and Dad sang very loud and very off key, but to them they were perfect.

After a couple mouthfuls of her favorite cake, Mom and Dad hand Rachel a small box. It's a brand new I-phone. Just what she wanted. "Thank you, thank you, thank you!" Rachel was very grateful for her parents.

That night while laying in bed, Rachel was texting all of her friends on her brand new phone.

# Chapter 2

September 2020 was as quiet and as normal as life could be. Rachel was doing well in school. She was acing her English class, she's passing government with the help of Taylor, and her favorite class would have to be creative writing with her friend Elijah. She would like to be an English teacher or an author one day.

One night while she was working on some calculus homework her dad was watching the five o'clock news. She really wasn't interested in the news. It was boring and it was always the same stories. Comes with living in a small town she guessed. A story finally caught her attention when the news anchor started to talk about a deadly virus working its way through China.

Forty two people have died so far. One patient that contracted the virus was an eight year old boy who displayed extreme signs of aggression. It was reported that he started to attack and bite people. Anyone he attacked was either injured or didn't make it.

"Kind of crazy what goes on on the other side of the world." Rachel's dad says from the comfort of his reclining chair. "Makes you wonder what our government would do in a situation like that."

Rachel really didn't want to think about what the government would do. Not that it would be boring, but because it scared her. Her dad always talked about how fucked up the government was.

An hour later Rachel's family eats dinner, then they watch reruns of *Cops* before everyone goes to bed.

******

October 2020 the first cases of the virus are reported in Washington State. A diplomat and his family were brought home from India. Their twin girls, fifteen, were experiencing headaches, nausea and fevers. A few days later they became violent. No one has heard from the family since.

Rachel keeps going to school. Everything in Royal, Colorado seemed normal. There were a couple kids missing from her American Sign Language class, and she had a substitute in creative writing. Everyone is saying it was just a really bad flu.

What kind of flu made people aggressive? Rachel wondered that almost everyday.

Three days later in AP English more than half the class was gone. The news was reporting that the CDC was recommending that if you had to go out in public to wear a mask. So Rachel, and whoever was left at the school, followed the recommendation.

Rachel and Zoe sat in class working on an assignment when a boy named Joey asked to go see the nurse. Rachel noticed he looked sweaty and was clutching his stomach.

Zoe turned around in her seat. "I heard kids were being sent to The Institute and put into isolation."

"They're just trying to figure out what's going on. I'm sure this will all be over soon." Rachel always tried to be optimistic.

"I heard once you're in The Institute you don't come out." A boy sitting next to Rachel chimed in.

A cold chill runs down Rachel's spine. Maybe this was more serious than she thought. She hopes she never ends up there.

# Chapter 3

Halloween was Rachel's family's favorite holiday. They go all out every year with decorations. Last year Rachel's dad even dug holes in their front yard to make it look like zombies were coming up from the ground. This year the decorations seemed to only stay inside. The family decorated some pumpkins for their front porch, but that was all for outside. The pumpkins will be there until they rot just like every year.

Rachel's mom went out and grabbed just a couple bags of candy. They weren't really expecting a lot of people this year with all the kids getting sick.

Rachel didn't trick or treat much anymore either. Since Halloween was on a Friday this year she was having a sleep over at Zoe's. They were going to stay up all night watching scary movies.

November was different too. There was a heaviness in the air and it seemed to drag and linger forever.  The month started off with an assembly at Rachel's school. Three of Rachel's teachers had passed away. Twenty teachers all together for the senior class.

It was hard for Rachel to wrap her head around. She knew most of her teachers had young children. They were husbands and wives, brothers and sisters. Were they all victims of this virus? Does that mean their kids were dead too?

That day Rachel had a substitute in Art 4. He told the class he was actually a physics major and the only art background he had was drawing stick figures. Needless to say, the class was unusually quiet that day.

Thanksgiving break wasn't the same either. Rachel's family usually went to her aunt's house a couple hours away in Utah. Her cousins who were younger than her weren't feeling good, so her family stayed home.

The Thanksgiving football game was supposed to be in Detroit this year. It was cancelled. The stadium was dead.

Come December, the only sound the TV made was a message from the CDC declaring a global health emergency.

******

By January 2021 there were two million cases reported. Half of those ended in death. The news wasn't really reporting anything else. Rachel was getting very scared. The flu doesn't kill this many people. What else could it be?

One day when Rachel's mom got back from the store she was as white as a ghost. She was shaking the whole time she was putting the groceries away.

"It was horrible." She told her family as she sipped on some tea to calm her nerves. "I was standing there grabbing one of the last loaves of bread, and a mom and her son were further down the aisle. He must have been ten, maybe twelve. He looked like death. Then all of a sudden..." Rachel's mom trails off staring into space.

"What happened, Mom?" Rachel asks her mom, trying to bring her back to reality.

"He just attacked her. Bit her right on the arm. He took a pretty good chunk. I saw his face. His eyes were wild like a crazed animal and his mouth was covered in blood. He was snarling and screaming, then he took off and just left his mom there."

"Thats horrible." Rachel's dad drapes his arm around his wife to comfort her.

"I tried to help her, but I couldn't stop the bleeding. It happened so fast. Then there were more screams. I grabbed what I had in the cart and got out of there."

"Maybe we can order the groceries to the house next time. Or I'll go with you to make sure you're safe." Rachel's dad tells his love.

Rachel's mom nods her head softly as she sips her tea. Mom was an ER nurse, she's seen it all. From accidental gunshot wounds during hunting season—to torn-off limbs from farming equipment. If she couldn't save people, if she was this scared, then something really is wrong out there.

That night on the news they reported about the attack at the grocery store. There were five deaths including the boy who was sick. A police officer just happened to walk into the store when he noticed the commotion. The sick boy was attacking a woman tearing into her side with his teeth. The officer unholstered his gun and unloaded it when the boy charged at him.

The officer said in an interview that he had never seen anything like it. He said the boy was acting like an animal with rabies.

Two children were bitten in the attack. They were being rushed to the hospital in critical condition.

# Rachel

## 2021

# Chapter 4

February 2021 all of the schools in Royal, Colorado were closed. They decided to do virtual learning, where the kids would stay home and learn from their computers. They thought this would slow down the spread of the virus.

Rachel's dad was laid off from his job. He was a repair foreman at a roofing company. One night Rachel heard him talking to one of his work buddies on the phone. Two of his kids were sick. They were seven and three.

Rachel and Zoe would text or call each other on their lunch breaks. Zoe told Rachel that she heard more kids were being sent to The Institute.

Rachel remembered that she saw a video on Facebook where a kid was being brought in by police officers. They had him restrained as he was kicking and screaming. He was snarling and snapping his teeth like a hungry animal.

At the end of the video he had bitten one of the officers on the neck. He pulled off skin; there was blood everywhere. He had tendons and veins hanging out of his mouth. The officer collapsed on the ground and then the video cut off.

Rachel almost thought the video was a fake until she recognized the kid in restraints. He was in her calculus class. His rust colored hair and freckled face gave him away.

One night around seven Rachel's mom came home from work. She was a shell of herself. She moved in slow, weak steps. Her eyes looked empty, there was no spark. No one got warm hugs that night.

******

A day in early March, Rachel was on the computer with her American Sign Language teacher. There were less kids on the video call then there were last time. Today's lesson was about the weather. They learned the signs for rain, sun, cloudy, wind, thunderstorm, snow, tornado and hurricane.

After twenty minutes of practice and silent conversation, Rachel could hear shuffling and a gurgling type sound coming from her computer. No one could decide where the sound was coming from until a kid appeared on the screen of her teacher. She had blood and snot running down her face, and what looked like vomit all over her shirt. She was making a low growling sound as she got closer to her mom.

Rachel's teacher jumped out of her seat to help her daughter. "Oh baby, you should be in bed. Let me help you. Kids I'll be..." Rachel's teacher turned back around to address the class but before she could finish her sentence her daughter latched onto her neck with her teeth and bit into her. Rachel could see flesh, muscle and tendons being ripped from her teacher's neck.

Rachel let out a scream that shook the whole house. Rachel's dad runs over from where he was standing in the kitchen and grabs his daughter into a hug as he sees the destruction on the screen. A kid on the screen is covered in fresh blood and is chewing on something. He sees Rachel's teacher fall to the ground with a chunk of her neck missing.

The kid looks down and falls to her knees. She leans over her mom and bites her again in her arm. The sickening squelch of flesh being torn and the crunch of bone makes Rachel's dad queasy. He reaches over and slams the laptop shut before he hears anymore.

Standing in the silence of the room while holding his crying daughter, Rachel's dad could only think of one thing: he needed to call his wife.

# Chapter 5

fter the incident of Rachel's last lesson, the school board decided to suspend all learning. Rachel's parents did their best to try to teach her themselves. Her dad taught her some basic math skills and had long talks with her about how the government works, or doesn't. While her mom was home she would teach her some science and things about the human body like immune systems and how red blood cells work.

Rachel's parents gave her the birds and the bees talk years ago, so she didn't need to learn that.

Mom would go to work and come home an empty shell. She would lock herself in their room and wouldn't come out for hours. A couple times she would hear her mom crying. Other times she would hear nothing. She wondered if her mom was just lying in bed in silence.

It took Rachel a couple days to not think about what she saw on her computer screen when her teacher got attacked. She couldn't imagine what her mom was seeing at work. And she had to see it almost every day.

Rachel and Zoe would have sleep overs at each other's houses periodically. Zoe thought it was kind of strange that Rachel's  parents were trying to teach her stuff. Zoe felt bad that her friend still had to learn on their time off. Rachel felt bad that Zoe's mom seemed to not give a fuck, but she didn't tell her friend that.

By the end of the month they all seemed to settle into a new normal. That was until Rachel saw the boy across the street get shot.

******

It was late afternoon on the last day of March when Rachel and her family heard a commotion outside. The sound of an ambulance filled the quiet neighborhood. It was stopped at the house across the street. Rachel knows there are two kids that live there. A boy around the age of twelve and his younger sister who was probably around seven or eight.

Their mom greeted the paramedics at the door with blood covered hands and a face full of tears. Rachel couldn't make out what she was saying. A couple seconds later a police cruiser pulled up.

They all disappeared inside the house and Rachel thought it was all over. They couldn't have been gone for more than a minute when a police officer comes out with a bleeding paramedic. The officer laid the paramedic down on the ground and applied pressure to her neck.

Another police officer comes out with the young boy in restraints, he was kicking and snapping his blood stained jaws just like the boy from her calculus class. His screams could be heard around the world.

The boy, much smaller and younger than the man restraining him, seemed to be overpowering the man. In the struggle he throws his head back and headbutts the officer in the nose. The officer loses his grip and the boy makes a bee line for the other officer on the ground.

He's on him in seconds and tears into his face with his teeth. The officer lets out a painful scream as flesh and muscle are pulled away. The other officer regains his composure and unholsters his weapon. He aims it at the thing attached to his friend's face. His voice is so loud Rachel can hear his rugged western accent with his commands.

The boy stands and turns to the officer holding his gun. His parents appear at the doorway, no doubt hearing all of the yelling. His mom screams at the sight of the officer on the ground who is now missing half of his face. The boy lurches toward the officer with his teeth still snapping.

Right before the boy makes it to the officer he unloads his weapon.

# Chapter 6

Rachel fell into a stage of depression come April. She rarely left her room. She stopped texting her friends. She even stopped eating, which was very unlike her. Her parents tried to comfort her the best they could, but even they can admit they don't know everything about parenting a teenage girl.

This might be something Rachel will have to figure out for herself.

Rachel's mom started working longer and longer shifts at the hospital. Sometimes she would already be asleep when Mom got home.  If she wasn't fully asleep yet she would hear her parents talking. One night she heard her mom say they converted a whole floor of the hospital just for the "special cases." That's what they started calling the kids who had the virus. She heard her mom say it wasn't like anything they've ever seen before and it scared her.

It scared Rachel too. She didn't want to see anymore blood and guts or death. So that gave her another reason to stay hidden in her room.

April 13 Rachel got a message from Zoe. It was Zoe's 17th birthday and she invited her out to a party at a boy's house just around the corner.

Rachel asked her parents if she could go. They said it didn't really seem like a good idea. It was an "unnecessary risk" as her mom put it.

Later that night Rachel snuck out of her house and met up with Zoe to go to the party.

******

Zoe told Rachel they were going to Zach's house. A boy Zoe knew from her math class. His parents were on a trip in Vienna, Austria for their wedding anniversary. They were expected home three days ago. They haven't returned, nor have answered any of his calls.

He was definitely taking advantage of the situation. Rachel only hoped that his parents were okay.

They get to the house and slip off their coats. The house is warm compared to the chill of the late April night and filled with teenagers drinking alcohol and playing beer pong. The girls see Taylor and Elijah in a big crowd and join them.

They dance and laugh for almost five hours. Rachel didn't like the taste of beer. She thought it tasted like piss. Though she never had tasted actual piss before, she thought it was an accurate description. One of the boys brought her another drink that tasted like grape even though it was labeled black cherry. She enjoyed that one and had a couple of those throughout the night.

A boy in the crowd of dancers came to the party with a fever and started to feel a little nauseous. He couldn't tell if it was just the alcohol making him sick or if he had a cold. His little brother bit him the other day on his leg and he was pretty sure it was infected. The little twirp probably gave him the flu or something. His fever was getting worse. He starts to sweat and get the chills. He pushes through the crowd and makes his way to the bathroom before he throws up all over the floor.

Unbeknownst to the kids outside dancing, drinking and flirting, the boy in the bathroom had passed out and will wake with a brand new personality.

Rachel looks at her phone and realizes the time. She should head home soon before her parents suspect anything.

A boy comes up behind her and grabs her shirt. She pushes him away, not really looking up at his face. He stretches his arms out again and grabs ahold of her. "Hey!" Rachel calls out exasperatedly. She looks up to confront her admirer and is met with a growl and a deep snarl across his face. He sinks his sharp jagged teeth into her, breaking the skin on her shoulder.

She pushes her attacker as hard as she can and he stumbles backwards into a table. He's completely hammered, she thought. He can't even stand straight. Biting someone really wasn't a good way to get their attention either. Damn, it hurts. Rachel goes to find her friends back in the crowd. She hears an ow and looks over her shoulder. She sees the same guy bite into someone else.

She finds Zoe and the boys as she holds onto her bleeding shoulder. "What happened to you?" Elijah asks her.

"Someone bit me." Rachel answers back revealing the teeth marks embedded into her skin.

"Jesus!" Taylor exclaims as he eyes the mark.

"Oh my god! Are you okay?" Zoe grabs Rachel by the arm.

"It hurts but I think I'm okay. I should go home now anyways. It's late." Rachel tells her friends.

"I'll go with you." Zoe tells Rachel and they wave goodbye to the boys.

Rachel hears a couple more ows as they make their way to the front of the house. They grab their coats and as they leave they start to hear screams coming from inside.

# Taylor

## 2020

# Chapter 7

Taylor couldn't wait for school to start. He hadn't seen his best friend Elijah all summer. Elijah's parents had the audacity to take him to Hawaii. What jerks.

There really wasn't much to do in Royal, Colorado during the summer. All of the cool stuff was for winter, like snowboarding and skiing. If one was feeling courageous enough, he could also ask a pretty girl to go ice skating. Girls seemed to like that. They call it romantic.

Taylor wasn't that courageous. Not when it came to girls.

Taylor played video games a lot by himself. Every now and again he would get a text message from Elijah. It was usually pretty girls in their bikinis at the beach. It made Taylor jealous.

Elijah was coming back the day before school started and Taylor couldn't wait to hear about everything he did. Taylor hoped to see more pictures of the pretty...sites.

The coolest thing Elijah already told him about was swimming with sharks. The coolest thing Taylor did this summer was beat level twenty of his video game.

******

Taylor had a good first day of school. He had English, Spanish 3, chemistry, and government with his friend Rachel. Talking about Rachel with his mom always made him blush.

Taylor and Elijah were going to sign up for cross country in the fall together and do lacrosse in the spring. They had their lives all planned out.

Taylor wished Rachel a happy birthday when he saw her in class today. He liked her smile and the way she laughed. He even started to worry about what he was going to wear when he saw her.

That night as Taylor was getting ready for bed he received a text from Rachel saying she got a new phone for her birthday. He wished it was just the two of them. Maybe he would finally tell her how he felt about her, but it was a group chat with Zoe and Elijah. He decided to wait. They stayed up a while talking about their days and Elijah's trip before falling asleep.

# Chapter 8

September was shaping up nicely for Taylor. He and Elijah were running cross country together and they're already looking to place first in the Division One Championship. Taylor's parents come to every race to cheer him on. He beat his last record by fifteen minutes.

Taylor would love to get a scholarship for running. His parents would appreciate that too.

One September night Taylor's dad was watching the five o' clock news. Taylor was doing his English homework at the kitchen table. His favorite section of the news was the sports center. Taylor's favorite hockey team was doing well this year. That's all that mattered to him.

Then a breaking news story came on. Something about a deadly virus in China. The news anchor said forty two people have died already. A young boy who had the virus apparently was acting aggressive and biting people.

"Get a load of this, Char." Taylor's dad calls out to his wife. His midwestern twang is ever prominent thanks to a couple Bud Lights.

"Those poor people." Taylor's mom responds from the kitchen. She's making her family's favorite dinner. Homemade lasagna with dinner rolls. "There's so many people over there. I'm surprised they don't have new diseases more often."

"That's what they want you to think. This is probably just another scare tactic so more people get the flu shot this year. It's just a big scam to profit from big pharma." Taylor's dad was a huge skeptic when it came to the news. He always told him to not believe everything you hear.

Taylor thinks his dad likes to watch the news just to give him something to bitch about.

"Just you wait." Taylor's dad adds. "The next thing they'll tell us to do is stay inside and that we're drinking too much milk."

"Okay, babe. Whatever you say." Taylor's mom looks at her son and does the crazy sign with her finger spinning around near her head.

Taylor couldn't help but to laugh out loud.

# Zoe

## 2020

# Chapter 9

Zoe knows she's different. She doesn't mind being different. It was better than being normal. She liked to box dye her hair black and her clothes reminded people of the 80's, back when Guns N' Roses were popular. She didn't really care what other people thought. She liked what she liked and it made her happy. Nothing else mattered to her.

Zoe's mom was kinda the same. Though Zoe's mom was labeled the town drunk. It bothered Zoe when she would hear people talk bad about her mom, but her mom didn't care. She always told her that there's always one person in a small town that gets made fun of. It just happens to be her. She would say they were just jealous of her. Zoe knew her mom was just trying to make her feel better.

Zoe's best friend never judged her or her mom. That's what she liked most about Rachel. She wasn't like all the other stuck up kids in town. She accepted Zoe and her mom just as they were.

Zoe knows her mom won't be winning any mom of the year awards but she still loved her all the same.

Zoe and Rachel spent a lot of time together this summer. Neither of their families could afford a vacation, and they were blessed that they lived right next door to each other. They would take turns having sleep overs at each other's houses, they would go to the mall and look at expensive things that they couldn't afford, and on nice days they would go to the pool and pretend they were on a far away island where the local hot guys would serve them drinks with tiny umbrellas in them. You know, normal teenage girl stuff.

Even with all the time they spent together, Zoe couldn't wait to see her friend more at school. They had a class together this year too which had them pretty excited.

******

Zoe had a good first day. She bought Rachel's favorite candy bar for her birthday gift. Rachel turned seventeen today. She knew it wasn't much, but her friend loved it.

Zoe never really talks about her days with her mom. By the time she gets home, her mom would normally be passed out on the couch with a bottle of scotch in her hand. Today was no different, except it was a bottle of brandy.

She made her way to her room where she spends most of her time. She turned on some music and did her homework.

Zoe got a text message later that night from Rachel saying that she got a new phone for her birthday. She was excited for her. They talked to Taylor and Elijah for a while too before they all went to sleep.

# Chapter 10

Zoe was doing pretty well in school. She was acing English, she had a couple B's, but the only class that was giving her trouble was chemistry. She hated science. She would be lucky if she passed with a C.

Her mom didn't really care about grades. She didn't really care about anything in Zoe's life. But Zoe cared. She wanted to go to college far, far, far away from here. Usually that took good grades.

She wants to go to film school in California and become a famous movie producer like Steven Spielberg or Ridley Scott. She wants to make the next big blockbuster horror movie.

A girl can dream.

One night in September Zoe was on the couch eating popcorn watching *Aliens* when the news interrupted one of her favorite movies.

A breaking news story flashes on the tv screen. The nightly news anchor said there was a new deadly disease sweeping through China. Forty two people have died so far from this new virus. The news anchor says they know of a little boy who contracted the virus and became  extremely violent. He started attacking and biting everyone around him. Anyone he attacked was either in critical condition or pronounced dead.

That's gnarly Zoe thought to herself. She wanted to call for her mom to watch the story with her, but she was in her room with a man that Zoe didn't know. So she decided it was better to just leave her alone.

******

Six months pass. School has been closed which gave Zoe more time at home. She saw her mom with more strange men. Some of them passed Zoe's coolness test, but she wasn't ready to call any of them dad yet. With the local bars closed down too, this was probably going to be the new normal for Zoe. She just wishes she wasn't home when they went behind a closed door.

She didn't like thinking about that.

They did online learning for a while. That stopped when some kids saw their teacher get attacked during their lesson. Later, Zoe found out that it was Rachel's class. She thought it would have been cool to see all gore, but Rachel apparently didn't handle it well.

Then one of the kids across the street got sick. Police officers came to their house and Zoe watched as they brought the young boy out. He was kicking and screaming like he was possessed. He had blood all over his mouth and he was snapping his teeth like a hungry animal.

He got loose from the officer restraining him and attacked another officer on the ground who was helping a paramedic. He bit half of his face off from what Zoe could see. He went back for the other officer but before he could attack the officer shot him dead.

Zoe didn't hear from Rachel for over a week after that. She wondered if her friend saw what happened to the boy across the street.

They needed to let off some steam and relax. On April 13 Zoe invited Rachel to go out with her on her birthday. She knew a boy who was having a party just around the corner. It was the perfect time for them to have some fun.

# Taylor

## 2021

## The Party

# Chapter 11

Taylor couldn't believe what he was seeing. His friends and classmates were being torn apart by a boy. By a monster.

The party was going so well. He was having a great time with his friends. He even got to dance with Rachel. Her smile and her laugh made him so happy. When he was with her it felt like they were the only two in the room. And then he wanted to kiss her. How do girls do that?

Rachel left after she said someone bit her on her shoulder. She showed them the bite mark. It looked painful. He felt so bad for her. He wanted to punch whoever did it. The boys thought maybe it was someone in a drunken stupor, but even for a drunk person biting someone was a little strange.

Then he saw him. Stumbling around with vomit running down his shirt. Blood on his teeth. Taylor thought maybe *he* was the one in a drunken stupor. Maybe he was hallucinating. Sadly he was not.

The boy quickly bites into three kids. Two on their shoulders, they both pushed him away as if he was just an annoyance, then the last one he got on his ankle when the second kid knocked him down.

It wasn't until the next attack that the kids realized something was horribly wrong.

******

The boy stalked forward and grabbed a girl by her long hair. Taylor was going to intervene and push the boy off of her when he bit into her face. The girl turned to see whoever was pulling on her hair and it gave him the perfect angle to sink his teeth into her cheek.

He pulls off skin and muscle. Blood vessels are exposed and broken causing blood to stream down her face. Her scream echoes through the house making the music seem quiet. She falls to the floor grasping  at the hole in her face.

A panic comes over the house and everyone makes a run for the door. Taylor is frozen with shock. The monster shuffles past as Taylor is knocked down to the floor ending up in the pile of the girl's blood that now stains the hardwood. He is kicked and stepped on as the kids run for their lives.

Another boy is knocked down to the floor across the room and Taylor watches as the monster stumbles to the ground and bites the boy on the leg. He can hear flesh being torn and the crunch of bone as the boy lets out a terrifying scream.

Elijah bends down and grabs Taylor by the arm releasing him from his trance. "Let's go, dude! We gotta get out of here!" Elijah helps him up and the two friends run out of the house and into the night leaving the door open as they flee.

# Rachel

2021

After The Party

# Chapter 12

After twenty seven years of waking up before dawn, Rachel's dad still wakes up before the sun. He takes the time to make his wife lunch to take with her to the hospital and he has taken a liking to making at home coffee. His wife has been working fourteen sometimes even eighteen hour shifts lately. This disease hasn't slowed down or has gotten any easier to deal with according to her.

They lost more staff members recently, so it's all hands on deck at the hospital. The sick kids keep attacking the nurses and doctors. Anyone who gets bitten succumbs to their injuries pretty quickly, his wife told him. They've been trying to keep everyone safe, putting the kids in restraints and giving them mouth guards, but sometimes they're just too fast and abnormally strong.

Rachel's dad was never a God-fearing man but ever since this sickness started he's been praying every night before bed. He doesn't know what he would ever do without his wife or daughter.

The coffee pot sings its sweet song to let Dad know it's ready. He makes his first cup of the morning with a yawn. He goes to sit in his recliner and turns on the morning news.

The Colorado Institute of Science has started to urge people to bring in anyone with flu-like symptoms: headaches, fever, nausea, and vomiting. That could be anyone right now Dad thinks as he sips his hot coffee. The Institute states that people who are sick with these symptoms could become violent and uncontrollable at any moment. The most important thing they say is to not let these people bite you. That might be a quick way for this virus to spread.

The Institute is promising top-notch medical care to anyone who is admitted and a promise to find a cure for this deadly disease. Dad sips his coffee and can only think about how the government plans to pay for all of that.

Just after five in the morning Dad hears a noise come from upstairs.

******

Rachel has never snuck out of the house before. Climbing out of her window then jumping off of the roof was the most exhilarating thing she's ever done. Now she just has to sneak back in.

Zoe helped boost her up onto the roof in front of her window. The bite on her shoulder was now making her arm sore to move. She gets to her window and clumsily pulls herself through. Her arm fails her half way through the window and she crashes to the floor.

She knows Dad is awake already. She saw the lights on downstairs. It's only a matter of time before he makes his way up here.

She stumbles to her bed and tucks herself in tight as if nothing had happened. She hears heavy footsteps coming up the stairs then down the hall.

Dad pokes his head into Rachel's room and sees his sleeping daughter just where he expected to see her, curled up in her bed. Dad slowly closes the door and his heavy footsteps move back down the hall. Dad checks the rest of the upstairs then returns to his chair satisfied with his findings, nothing. Maybe the noise came from outside.

Rachel lays in her bed, quiet and dark. She's overcome with guilt as she cries herself to sleep.

# Taylor/Elijah

## 2021

## After The Party

# Chapter 13

Four houses down Taylor sits unnaturally still in Elijah's room as he watches with wide eyes as his friend paces back and forth. In contrast to Taylor, Elijah can't seem to sit still. His heart is racing, his chest feels tight. Is he having a heart attack? He's only seventeen. He rakes his fingers through the messy textured mop on top of his head. Both of the boys are covered in cold sweat and their complexions have gone extremely pale, ashen.

Taylor drops his head between his knees, afraid he might throw up. He wipes the sweat off his forehead with the sleeve of his sweater. He moves his long blonde bangs away and checks for a fever. No fever. What the hell is wrong with him? He's never felt this way before. Unsure, insecure, not safe.

"What the hell was that, man?" Elijah breaks the silence with a shaky voice. "Was he drugged? Was he high? What the fuck, man!"

Taylor shakes his head, slowly. Not looking up he replies, "I don't know, dude. Did you see it? He bit her face off dude. O-f-f. Off." Taylor's voice trembles, tears start to form around his eyes.

"I saw it, dude. Was that the new sickness everyone has been talking about?"

Taylor shrugs his shoulders.

In the darkness of the room the boys jump out of their skins when they hear more faint screams coming from outside. Neither of the boys know what to do next.

******

Elijah's little brother sleeps in his room just down the hall. His breathing is labored. Every breath is raspy and wheezy. He had a play date with his friend yesterday. It ended abruptly when his friend bit him on his hand. He cried and screamed. His friend wouldn't let him go.

Once they got home his mom saw the teeth marks on his hand. She bandaged it up after cleaning it with peroxide. He got some tasty ice cream to make him feel better and got to watch cartoons until bed time.

In the comfort of his bed his head pounds against his skull. His fever is silently climbing higher and higher. His tummy hurts. He feels like he might throw up. His little body is numb and sore, he doesn't think he'll make it to the bathroom in time.

The little boy begins to panic as his breathing becomes rapid and shallow. He starts to gasp. He can't get enough air. He's scared and wants his mom. She'll know what to do. He tries to call for her but nothing comes out. He struggles to sit up in bed. He forces his little legs to move and stands up to get to his door. He takes a couple little steps before he throws up all over his floor.

Oh no, he thinks. Mom and Dad are going to be upset. He almost makes it to his door when his little world goes dark and he collapses on to the floor.

# Rachel

## 2021

## 7hrs After The Bite

# Chapter 14

achel lays in her bed, feverish and pale. She shivers violently as heat radiates from her body. Her head feels like it could explode at any moment from the amount of pressure on her brain. Her unsettled stomach makes her mouth water, the threat of vomit looming closer and closer.

The sun is high in the sky. Rachel must have slept until noon. Her head is foggy, she must have lost concept of time. Her body is lethargic. Her muscles are sore and weak.

There's a knock at the door but Rachel is too weak to get up and open it.

Dad's voice is soft and gentle as he enters her room. Rachel doesn't turn to face him. "Hey, honey. How are you? I haven't seen you all day. Are you okay?"

Rachel lets out a moan between raspy breaths.

"Alright, kiddo. I'll leave you alone. I'll be downstairs if you need anything." Dad slowly closes the door, careful not to make any sound.

Dad has been through this before. It must be that time of the month again. Over the years Dad has learned the hard way how to deal with a teenage girl. It's just best to leave Rachel alone. She'll come down when she wants something to eat.

The day goes on. Day turns into night. Dad hasn't seen any sign of Rachel. Laura should be home soon. She can poke the sleeping bear.

*****

It's just after eight when Laura arrives home. The drive through town makes the place look deserted. All of the stores are still closed. They haven't been able to order pizza in over seven months. That was Laura's favorite comfort food. She would kill for just one slice right now.

The shifts at the hospital are slowly sucking her soul out. She's getting used to seeing the kids act like wild animals but she'll never get used to seeing her friends and coworkers being ripped apart. She has a theory that maybe instead of a sickness there's a new drug that is going around. Something that alters brain chemistry.

Royal, Colorado had a problem with cocaine about two years ago. If something is increasing their heart rates or giving them abnormal heart rhythms, then they aren't getting enough blood flow to their brains. If that happens they could just be going crazy from lack of oxygen. She knows it might be a long shot but they don't have a lot of evidence to state otherwise.

As she gets out of her car she sees a couple of silhouettes in the distance moving slowly down the street. One of them stumbles and falls. It clumsily picks itself back up and starts to shuffle down the road again. It's too dark to see who it is. It's probably just some drunk teenagers.

She remembers what it was like to be young and care free. She decides to leave them alone.

Inside, Laura walks into the wonderful smell of pasta and meatballs. Ryan and Rachel must have already eaten.

Laura sees her husband in his favorite spot watching their favorite ghost hunting show. The host of the show is a guy named Zak. She walks up behind Ryan and gives him a kiss on his cheek. "Hey, baby. How was your day?"

"Hey, babe. It was fine." Ryan says between a mouthful of meatballs.

"Thanks for making dinner, baby. It smells great." Laura puts her bag away and starts  to get a bowl of food ready for herself. "Where's Rachel? Did she eat already?"

Ryan shrugs his shoulders. "I'm not sure. She's been in her room all day. I think it's that time of the month again."

Laura rolls her eyes. "Okay. Well, I'll go check on her before I sit down with you."

"Godspeed!" Ryan calls to his wife.

Laura makes her way up the stairs and heads to Rachel's room. It's really not like her to go without eating. Especially during that time of the month. Rachel should be downstairs in the kitchen eating all of their snacks. Laura reaches her daughter's door and knocks three times.

"Hey, honey. It's Mom. Is it safe to come in?" Laura waits a minute. No response. She slowly and carefully opens the door to the bear's den.

A pungent smell of rotting meat takes over Laura's nose. She sees her daughter curled up in her bed. "Hey, honey. Are you okay?" Laura reaches her daughter's bedside and puts a hand on her forehead. Her daughter feels like she's on fire. Laura notices her breathing is labored and shallow. She rolls her over and sees nasty vomit all over her face and bed sheets. Her face is pale, her lips are blue.

"RYAN!!" Laura wails into the night. The image of her daughter looking almost dead in her bed will be forever etched into her mind.

# Zoe

## 2021

## After The Party

# Chapter 15

Zoe had to help Rachel sneak back into her house after the party. For Zoe, all she had to do was open the front door. Just after five in the morning she walks into her house, still dark and quiet. The living room is littered with empty bottles and beer cans. Her mom is on the couch fast asleep. She probably never even noticed Zoe was gone.

Zoe makes her way to the kitchen. She might be able to hold her liquor, but if she doesn't eat something soon she'll turn into a monster.

Zoe settles on a bowl of cereal made with spoiled milk. She makes her way upstairs and sleeps like the dead until late in the afternoon.

Zoe wakes up convinced she's allergic to the sun. The bright light burns her eyes. Her head spins and pounds against her skull. Yesterday's events are a little blurry, but she remembers leaving early with Rachel. She still has the same clothes on and a bowl of cereal is by her bed. She looks around her room, nothing is out of place. She looks under her bed, no one is hiding. Everything seems good.

As normal as any other day, a shower and a change of clothes will probably help her wake up.

******

After her shower Zoe makes her way downstairs. Her mom is gone. Hopefully she's at the store. The living room is still a mess. Zoe decides to hangout upstairs. If she doesn't see the mess, then it doesn't exist. Zoe sits on her bed. She sends Rachel a message, wondering how her friend is doing.

Seconds turn into minutes. Minutes turn into hours. Zoe hasn't heard from Rachel or seen her mom all day. Zoe got so bored she actually cleaned up the living room.

Just after eight, Zoe sits in front of the TV watching *How to Catch a Serial Killer*. She sees the bright blinding glow of headlights coming down the street. She takes a deep breath hoping that it's Mom coming home. They drive past her house. She lets her breath out and a wave of sadness comes over her. She looks out of the window and sees the car pull into Rachel's house. It's Rachel's mom.

She looks off into the distance like something or someone caught her attention and Zoe follows her gaze. In the darkness she can barely make out a couple of figures shuffling down the road. Zoe goes back to her show, still holding onto a hope that her mom will show up soon too.

Not much later Zoe hears another commotion outside. She goes to the window to see what it is. She sees movement at Rachel's house. She can make out Rachel's mom scrambling for the driver door of her car. Rachel's dad comes out of their house holding her best friend in his arms. Rachel doesn't seem to be moving. Zoe watches as he climbs into the back seat and they speed right past her house, around the corner, then into the night.

# Elijah

## 2021

## After The Party

## Chapter 16

Elijah's parents were some of the lucky ones. They get to keep working while everything is shut down. Elijah's dad is the new police chief of Royal, Colorado. After over twenty years of service and exceptional leadership skills, Matt finally got the promotion of a lifetime. He might not be a patrol officer anymore, but now he gets to use his skills in other ways to keep his community safe.

Ashley was the best paralegal in northern Colorado. After a decade of teaching fourth grade math she needed a change of scenery. She thought her high-stakes negotiation skills and organization would be a good fit for the work. She loved her new job. She was very good at it.

With Elijah home from school they relied on him to watch his little brother. Most of the time Elijah didn't mind. They would eat snacks, watch movies, then play Minecraft together most days. Elijah prided himself on his grilled cheese making skills. He thought he would put that on his resume one day.

However, this day was different. Elijah and Taylor barely got any sleep. The chaos of the night gave them nightmares anytime they closed their eyes. When Elijah's parents said goodbye in the morning they thought the boys were just waking up, but in reality they never really went to bed.

In his tired, distraught, disconnected state he forgot about his one and only duty: check on his brother.

******

The boys were going down the rabbit hole. They were searching on Elijah's computer all day about different drugs, or what could cause a person to bite another person. Nothing really came close to what they saw that night.

The boys weren't hungry. Which was weird for teenage boys who usually ate everything in sight. *Everything*. They never left their room. Neither did Elijah's brother, Benjamin.

Day turned to night again. The boys finally drifted off to sleep: Elijah in his bed, and Taylor in the computer chair. They startled awake when they heard the door open, it was Elijah's mom.

The realization that Elijah hasn't checked on Ben all day finally hits him.

"Hi, boys!" Mom calls from the doorway. "How was your day?"

Elijah and Taylor appear at the top of the steps. "It was fine, Mom." Elijah calls back nervously.

"Your brother wasn't too much to handle today?"

"Nope. He was perfect. He hardly left his room." Elijah lies through his teeth.

Mom raises her eyebrows suspiciously. "Okay. I'll go check on him."

Elijah's mom walks up the steps and passes Elijah and Taylor to get to Ben's room. Elijah starts to pray silently that Ben is alive and just asleep in his bed.

Mom knocks on the door three times. "Hey, Benji. It's Mom. I'm coming in." Ashley pushes open the door and a nauseating, rancid smell fills the hallway. She doesn't see Ben in his bed or playing on the floor. "Ben?" The air in the room is heavy with the smell of death. There's a stain on his carpet that wasn't there before. Ashley looks around and spots Ben in the corner facing the wall.

"Hey, Ben. What are you doing, baby?" Ashley approaches her son and right before she reaches him his little body turns around and reveals a little face covered in blood and vomit. His eyes are dark and sunken. "Oh my God!" Mom yells out running to grab her baby boy. "What's the matter, baby?"

A low growl emerges from Ben as Elijah and Taylor step into the room covering their noses. Before anyone else can say anything, Ben latches onto his mom's throat. Ben bites and shakes like a hungry shark ripping apart a seal. Ben lifts his head pulling away skin, veins, and muscle as his mom falls to the floor, bleeding out. Her jugular vein has been severed; blood squirts all over the room.

The boys let out screams that fill the quiet night sky. Ben locks eyes with them, flesh and veins hanging out of his mouth. They turn and run out of the house leaving little Ben behind, chewing on a piece of his mother.

# Elijah/Taylor

## The Following Night
## After The Party

## Chapter 17

The house down the street should be empty, the boys thought. All of the party-goers ran for their lives, and they were pretty sure Zach's parents weren't coming home. No one should be there. The boys ran for the house and got to the front door that was still open.

The house is eerily quiet. There was dirt on the floor from knocked-over potted plants and tables that were on their sides. If you didn't know the horror that happened here you would say it probably was just a break in. Then they saw it, turning the corner through the archway of the living room were pools and pools of blood.

Pieces of hair, ripped clothing, and little bits of flesh and brain matter were scattered throughout the area. Taylor tries to keep his composure in front of his friend, but he is unsuccessful. He adds a pool of vomit to the disaster.

Elijah walks ahead while Taylor finishes puking. The girl who had her face bitten off is gone and the boy who got bit on his leg. Elijah didn't know what he expected to see, but the deserted house in its current state was kind of freaking him out. He was getting goosebumps and the hair on his arms was standing straight up.

Something wasn't right. He could feel it.

Before Elijah could get Taylor's attention, he sees his friend fall to the ground with a monster on top of him.

*****

Taylor was fighting for his life. The boy from the party must have been hiding around the corner. Taylor didn't hear him sneak up on him when he was grabbed. He turned and was face to face with snapping teeth. He was trying to push the boy off of him when he lost his footing and fell backwards onto the floor with the monster still attacking him.

The boy's rancid breath and smell of decaying skin was going to make Taylor sick again. Taylor closes his eyes and pushes with all his might to try and get this thing away from him. The boy lets out an angry roar, spitting saliva and bits of flesh onto Taylor's face. Yep, he was going to get sick again.

Taylor was pretty sure he could hear teeth breaking from the force the boy was snapping his jaws together. Inch by inch the monster was getting closer. Right as it seemed the predator was going to get its prey, a loud *snap* echoes through the house—and the monster falls to the floor.

Elijah had grabbed the toaster from the kitchen counter and whacked the monster in the head to save Taylor. Taylor stands up and wipes his face with his sleeve. "Thanks, dude."

"No problem." Elijah and Taylor stand together in a stunned silence for a second, taking in what just happened. A noise from behind them makes them jump.

A monster is crawling at them from down a dark hallway. It starts to moan and screech as it pulls its body closer to the boys. Taylor recognizes his face. It's the boy he saw get bit on the leg. He remembers he heard snapping and bone crunching. The boy's leg must be broken.

Elijah and Taylor start to back peddle out of the room and make their way back to the front door. They have to swerve out of the way when the girl with half of her face missing lunges at them from around the staircase.

They run down the street towards Rachel's house. Taylor couldn't believe it. He finally figured it out. They were running away from zombies.

# Police Chief Bahrke

# Chapter 18

Police Chief Bahrke of the Royal Colorado Police Department was late getting home. His days at the station were getting increasingly difficult. The amount of unrest this small town has seen in such a short time was unprecedented. The most surprising of it all was that the unrest involved children.

The morale in the station was fading quickly. The loss of a handful of officers in just a couple months was weighing heavily on his shoulders. His leadership skills that got him this position were being tested. This situation; however, was something they never studied for. The death of more officers only added more weight to his chest. On top of everything else, he was commanding his officers to shoot children.

The RCPD has some of the best officers in the country. They were the best trained, the best disciplined, and the most hard working group of men and women this town has ever seen. The majority of the force consisted of men and women who have families back home, young children. Under normal circumstances most of the time the officers didn't need to use deadly force. A quick zap from a taser or the threat of pepper spray usually got the job done. This new onslaught of attacks seemed to be anything but normal.

Children as young as five were biting and tearing flesh from bone. Their strength and relentless determination was unlike anything they have ever seen. How do you justify that in your head? How do you make someone feel better after killing a child?

Police Chief Bahrke has two sons of his own. He doesn't know what he would do if he ever had to make that choice. Could he do it? How do you shoot a child?

Making the last turn into his neighborhood, he sees two silhouettes running across the street. They start to pound and scream on a neighbor's door. His eyes adjust and as he gets closer he can make out his oldest son and his best friend in a state of panic.

******

Elijah and Taylor bombard Rachel's door with their fists. Their calls and screams have gone unanswered. The house is dark and quiet. Too quiet.

The blinding rays of headlights illuminate the boys. They stop and turn to see who's pulling in.

"Elijah? Taylor?" A gruff abrupt voice calls them from the dark.

"Dad? Dad!" Elijah calls back. The boys run up to the police chief.

"What's going on? Does anyone need help?" Chief Bahrke asks.

The boys tell Chief what happened at the party and what they saw running back into the house. The chief hesitates for a second, debating on whether to believe the boys or not. Teenage boys can have over active imaginations with their violent video games and such. The look in their eyes says they're serious and with his training he can tell the boys are telling the truth.

"Where are Mom and Ben?" Chief asks his son.

Elijah, with tears running down his face, looks at his dad and with a broken sob tells him that Mom and Ben are dead. Elijah states that Ben must have been sick and he admitted to not watching him like he should have been.

When Mom got home she went to check on Ben and that's when Ben attacked her, ripping out her throat.

Chief Bahrke's world comes crumbling down around him. His chest tightens after his heart skips a beat. "Is there anywhere else for you boys to go? I want to go to the house and check it out for myself."

The boys point down the street. Just two doors down their friend Zoe sits in her house still waiting for her mom to come home.

# Rachel

## 15hrs After The Bite

# Chapter 19

Rachel is ripped from her dad's arms the second they pull up to The Institute. Two men in hazmat suits grab her, one on each arm. A smaller lady approaches her and gags her before she can bite anyone.

"We need to get her in now," Rachel hears the lady say. "Before she fully turns."

Rachel's head is pounding as she tries to force her eyes to focus. Her legs are dragging against the hard concrete path leading to the entrance. She tries to move them but it's too painful. Her body seems to be trying to fight off whatever disease is coursing through her.

The concrete path turns to cold tile floor as Rachel is dragged past a welcome desk. She turns her head slightly to the right and sees her parents watching her through the floor to ceiling windows that make up the front wall of the building. Mom is crying. Dad has his finger in the lady's face. He must have some choice words for her.

The men holding onto Rachel stop at an elevator and one of them hits the button. Before they step on, Rachel's dad runs up to one of the windows. "We'll be back for you, baby! We'll be back—I promise!" Dad yells through the glass.

Rachel wants to call back to her dad. To tell him everything will be okay, but it hurts to breathe. She doesn't think she could talk very well right now. The two men drag her into the elevator and Rachel's parents disappear from her view.

******

The elevator opens and Rahcel is pulled around a corner. The hallway has five rooms; two on each side, and one room straight ahead that she can see. The fluorescent lights in the ceiling are softly humming.

The men haul her down the hallway. She almost feels like a dog who's been taken to the pound. A red flash catches her eye to the right. She sees a boy. At least it looks like a boy. His face is covered in blood and it's contorted into a snarl. He's clawing at the window that lines the front of his room. His rust colored hair glowing under the light.

The room to the left has a person in it wearing another hazmat suit. They're pushing around a mop. Rachel can see blood smears covering the walls.

Rachel comes to a stop at the room at the end of the hallway. One of the men uses a key card. The door turns green and clicks open. They pull Rachel inside and sit her down. One man tells her she can remove her gag once they leave the room. She sits in silence except for the hum of the lights after the men leave.

Twenty minutes later someone puts a tray of food through a slit in Rachel's door. She's overcome with a ravenous hunger and she goes to devour the plate. The second it hits her stomach it comes back up. It did nothing to fill her up. She's almost craving something else. The smell of meat or...flesh?

Rachel ends up convulsing on the floor later that night.

# Police Chief

# Bahrke

# Chapter 20

Shadows from the dark are slowly approaching Chief Bahrke and the boys. Moaning and screeching the closer they get to their prey. The snapping of their teeth echoing in the night.

Chief Bahrke aims his 9mm handgun with a shaky hand. He's readying his conscience to shoot at anything that comes too close.

Elijah and Taylor are banging on their neighbor's door trying to get her attention. The noise is drawing in more monsters. A heartbeat later Zoe opens the door, surprised to see her friends and the chief.

Chief Bahrke pushes the boys inside then slams the door. He holsters his 9mm and takes a deep breath. "Is your mom home, Zoe?" Chief asks. In a small town like Royal, Colorado everyone knows everyone, and everyone knows the chief.

"No, I haven't seen her all day." Zoe answers the chief. Her wide eyes can't hide her shock.

"Okay, everyone listen." The chief instructs the kids. "I'm going out to check on Ben and Mom. Everyone wait here and do not open this door until I come back or Zoe's mom comes home. Understood?"

The kids instinctively all answer, "Yes, sir."

"I'll be back." Before Chief leaves he looks at his son. He doesn't say anything but Elijah knows the look well. He knows his dad loves him. The chief is just too stubborn to say it.

Chief Bahrke unholsters his 9mm, opens the door, then disappears into the night.

******

Chief quickly realizes he needs to start hitting the gym again. His new desk job doesn't call for much running. These people, or things, move pretty slow so he can easily dodge them. He didn't need to use his gun.

He passes the house where the boys said they had the party. He runs by a girl who was missing half of her face and a boy who was pulling himself through the grass. If they weren't trying to claw at him or bite him, he would have stopped to help them.

He reaches his house and tries to prepare himself for what he might see.

"Ben? Ashley?" The chief calls out but doesn't receive a response. He does his training and clears the first floor. He doesn't find Ben or his wife. The boys said they were upstairs. Maybe he was just stalling, afraid of what he'll find.

Chief makes his way up the stairs, slowly. "Ben? Ashley? Honey?" He calls out again. No response.

He clears the master bedroom, then Elijah's room. He hears a sickening squelch and tearing coming from down the hall. Ben's room.

He cautiously approaches the room. His hands are shaking and sweating. The chief makes it to the end of the hall and the noises grow louder. He turns into little Ben's room and sees what he thinks is his son. "Ben?"

Little Ben looks up, smelling fresh meat. Blood, flesh, and veins covering his little face. A low growl comes out of Ben. Chief is frozen in shock. What has become of his family?

Chief sees a lady on the floor. He recognizes the ring on her finger. It's his wife. His beloved Ashley. His heart shatters and a sickening feeling takes over him. He realizes what Ben has done. What Ben has turned into.

Ben screeches as he lunges forward toward his dad. The chief raises his gun preparing to defend himself.

# Ryan/Laura

# Chapter 21

"How was your day, baby?" Ryan asks his daughter who was sitting in her car seat in the back.

"It was good, Daddy. I made a new friend!" A bubbly, bouncy, and very animated little Rachel answers back.

"That's great, baby! What's their name?"

"Her name is Zoe and we're best friends! We made each other bracelets!" Little Rachel holds up her hand to show off a small plastic rope with beads on it tied to her wrist.

"That's great, honey. I'm so happy for you!"

"Do you have a best friend, Daddy?" Little Rachel asks very seriously. Do grown-ups have friends? Rachel doesn't see a bracelet on Daddy's hand. Does he not have a best friend?

"I do." Dad answers cheerfully.

"Who is it?!" Little Rachel gasps in surprise.

"Mommy, of course."

"Mommy? But she's your wife." Little Rachel tilts her head in confusion.

Dad can't help but to chuckle. "That's exactly why she's my wife. She makes me happy and we have fun together. Just like you and your friends."

"Oh, but you don't have a bracelet." Little Rachel tilts her head the other way, still confused. "How do you know you're best friends without bracelets?"

"Well, Mommy gave me another very special gift."

"What is it?!" Little Rachel asks excitedly.

"She gave me you. You're my special gift." Dad says looking at his daughter through the rearview mirror.

Little Rachel giggles happily. "Love you, Daddy!"

"I love you my precious girl. Now, let's get home so you can tell Mommy about your new friend!"

"Okay, Daddy!"

Rachel's sweet laughter drifts away as Ryan is pulled back to reality. He's in the car with Laura. It's quiet. There is no laughter. There is no little Rachel in the back seat. He looks over at Laura who has been crying the whole way home. "Don't worry, honey. Rachel will come home. She'll make it. She's strong. She'll fight it." Ryan grabs Laura's hand and squeezes it, trying to reassure his wife.

The rest of the way home is quiet. Ryan keeps having flashbacks of Rachel's childhood: her first time crawling, her first time walking, her first word, her first trip to the beach, all of her firsts. He was always so proud of her. Thinking about all those good times starts to make him cry. Would he ever see his daughter again? His precious little girl. His special gift.

Making the last turn onto their street, he sees something odd. A patrol car is parked in front of Rachel's friend's house, the one with the nose ring.

*****

Through tear stained eyes Laura is forced to face her new reality. She has seen what this horrible disease does to people. It changes them, forces them to act like rabid animals. Snarling, growling, and snapping their teeth. Just waiting to bite onto something—or someone.

Something gnaws at her in the back of her mind. How did her daughter get sick? If this was drug related she was pretty confident Rachel didn't do anything like that. That theory is less likely now that Laura thinks of it. Kids as young as five were being brought into the hospital. They shouldn't be on any drugs. Unless they were getting into hidden stashes. There were so many though all at once. So, so many. It doesn't make sense.

Laura remembers some of her patients had visible bite wounds on them. Could that be how it spreads? She didn't see any bite marks on Rachel though. At least she doesn't remember seeing any. If it's not that could it be airborne? More people would probably be sick now though if that was the case. The most bizarre thing is that it only seems to turn young people into those crazy animals. None of her co-workers who were attacked survived.

So how is Rachel sick? Her only baby girl. Will she turn into an animal too? Will she survive? Will she ever see her baby girl again? She can't shake the image of her baby girl turning into a wild animal out of her head.

What would be worse? Seeing her daughter turn into someone she doesn't even recognize, or seeing her baby girl dead? That question haunts her the rest of the drive home.

Ryan makes the last turn onto their street and Laura can see a patrol car parked in front of Zoe's house. She hopes Zoe and her mom are okay.

Getting out of the car, Laura can start to make out silhouettes moving in the darkness. They're moving slowly and clumsily. She hears grunts and moans.

Something about this night sends a chill down her spine. The stationary patrol car still running, the slow moving silhouettes, and the noises she hears seem wrong.

Something about this night feels like it will be a very, very long night.

# Police Chief Bahrke

# Chapter 22

hief Bahrke charges his way back to his son and his friends. The image of his dead wife and the thing that used to be his little Ben will terrorize him until his last breath.

The creatures outside are no longer young children experiencing life for the first time, they are threats. As a police officer, it is his duty to eliminate any and all threats to the community.

The *pop* of his 9mm echoes through the night as the bullets tear through the shoulder and chest of one of the things that was lurking next door. The thing didn't go down. It wasn't even fazed from the holes in its chest. It lunged at Matt. Its arms outstretched. Its mouth was open, prepared to latch onto him at any moment. Another *pop* from Matt's 9mm and the thing finally goes down.

Matt's training taught him to shoot to kill. The chest was normally the go to area. When that didn't work,

Matt could only think of one other place to shoot—the head.

The noise Matt was making drew more creatures to him and he took them out one by one on his way back.

******

Zoe, Taylor, and Elijah were all waiting for the chief to get back. They watched as he disappeared around the corner, dodging the monsters. They waited for what felt like an eternity. Some of the monsters turned to follow the chief, the others continued to slowly creep forward.

Drifting in and out of sleep, the kids were jolted awake from *pops* of gun fire. They quickly crowded the window, hoping to spot the source of the commotion outside. Chief comes into view and he's aiming his gun firing at anything that gets in his way.

Elijah didn't know what he was expecting, but seeing just his dad come around the corner gave him a sickening feeling in his stomach. His mom and Ben really were gone. They aren't coming back.

Chief takes out the last of the monsters closest to the house and the kids meet him at the door.

"Dad!" Elijah calls out as the chief comes through the door.

Chief embraces his son. Through tears and heavy sobs Matt tells his son that Mom and Ben are gone. Ben wasn't Ben anymore he said. Both him and Mom are in a better place.

"We should all stay here tonight." Chief tells the kids. "Ill go back out in the morning and have a better look around. I'll see if I can figure out what's going on. In the meantime, why don't you kids get some rest? I'll keep watch."

The kids nod in agreement. With tired eyes all of the kids find places to crash. The chief finds a chair and sits guard in front of the door. His 9mm ready for any movement coming towards the house.

No more kids were going to die on his watch. If anything came through that door they would have to get through him first.

# Ryan/Laura

## A New Day

# Chapter 23

It was a long and anxious night for Laura and Ryan. Dwelling in sadness and unknowing, they didn't sleep an ounce. The night seemed to drag on. They were slowly and quietly suffering, not knowing what was happening to their daughter. The slow, agonizing wait for dawn was draining and exhausting for their souls.

While sleep eluded them, they sat down with cups of hot coffee. Waiting for any news, praying it wasn't bad.

In the silence of their home, the jarring *pop* of gunfire pulls them out of their depression. *Pop pop*. They look at each other surprised. Gunfire is not a normal sound they hear in Royal, Colorado.

*Pop.*

Curiosity gets the better of them and they walk to their front room to look out of the windows. There are more slow moving silhouettes than before. Then they see someone come around the corner. He lifts his arms up and they hear more *pops*. The silhouettes start to drop to the ground.

As the man gets closer, the *pops* grow louder. More silhouettes drop that were closer to the houses. He clears the sidewalk and enters Zoe's house.

"I think that was Matt." Ryan states to his wife. "Did we just watch Matt kill someone?"

"Or something." Laura answers back. The little color she had left over draining from her face. Maybe the things outside aren't people after all.

******

Sunlight creeps up over the mountains slowly. The rays of light eerily illuminating the dead bodies littering the ground. Their faces frozen with permanent snarls and covered with human flesh. If they were lucky enough to catch a meal.

Laura and Ryan plan to see their daughter today at The Institute. Unaware of anything that has happened there. They only believe what The Institute has promised them. Top-of-the-notch medical care and a cure.

With no news from The Institute during the night, they hope that's a good sign. Hopefully their Rachel has pulled through.

Not wanting to waste any daylight, Laura and Ryan gather their things and make their way outside. What they see stops them dead in their tracks. Bodies covering the street. All shot in the head.

A noise from next door startles them, making them jump. Matt appears from Zoe's garage wearing a scarf around his face and carrying a shovel.

"Matt?" Ryan calls out.

Matt, hearing his name, turns and sees Ryan and Laura. They looked shocked and tired. Matt makes his way over to them wondering if they need any help.

"Hey, guys. Everyone okay over here?"

"What the hell is going on?" Ryan gestures to the ground covered in bodies.

"I'm not sure." Matt replies honestly. "Whatever is going on is making people aggressive. My team has multiple reports of sick people attacking and biting. I've seen it myself." Matt trails off looking out into space—thinking of his sweet Ashley and little Ben.

"That's what we were seeing at the hospital too." Laura agrees. "No one has given us a cause or how to treat it."

"How is Rachel doing?" Matt asks.

"We were actually just on our way to see her." Ryan tells him. "She got sick and we took her to The Institute last night."

"I'm so sorry. I hope she pulls through. Maybe some people will be immune to whatever the hell this is." Matt gestures to the ground. He hopes to reassure his neighbors that maybe their daughter will be okay.

"Thank you." Ryan replies. "How are you guys? What are you doing next door?"

"I'm keeping watch over Zoe, Elijah, and Taylor. Something happened at our house—it isn't safe. So I'm just trying to do my job. Keep people safe."

"What happened?" Laura asks concerned.

They notice Matt dropping his head and his big frame shifts uncomfortably. The big guy is trying not to cry. "Ashley and Ben are dead. I'm going back home to bury them."

Laura and Ryan gasp in shock. "What happened?" Ryan asks.

"Ben was sick. We didn't know what would happen. He changed. He wasn't Ben anymore. Ashley got home before me and she must have gone upstairs to check on him. He must have attacked her when she went into his room."

Laura and Ryan immediately look at each other. Their worst fear is realized. They take off back to their car. They didn't mean to be rude to Matt, they respect him, but Rachel needs them. If Rachel does have this disease they don't want her to be alone and scared. They certainly won't let her die being some sort of science experiment in a hospital.

# Ryan/Laura

# Chapter 24

The ride to The Institute was quiet. The occasional monster was roaming down the road. Laura and Ryan weren't sure what to call them. Were they dead? Were they alive? They weren't sure. Monster seemed to be a good fit.

They were just stumbling around looking almost lost. Laura wonders if they were trying to find home again. Maybe they really were lost. Would they be lost forever? Trying to find their parents. Trying to find their ways back home. It broke Laura's heart.

Was the only way to end their pain to shoot them in the head? Someone has to know what's going on. Someone has to find a cure. What would this world be without children?

Laura would gladly take this sickness from her daughter so Rachel could be healthy and live out her life.

She prays with all of her strength that she will have the chance to make her daughter better. She prays that Rachel is okay and that all of this will just be a bad dream in the end.

The Institute comes into view and a wave of urgency and concern comes crashing down over Laura and Ryan.

Their stomachs are in knots. Ryan was almost blue in the face from not breathing. The anticipation of seeing his daughter was killing him. His heart was beating so fast he thought it was about to explode.

He didn't want Rachel to be alone, but he was terrified of what they might see. If it wasn't for the adrenaline coursing through his body he would probably just break down this very second. He promised Rachel they would be back. He always keeps his promises.

Daddy is here Rachel. Daddy is coming for you. Daddy will keep you safe.

******

Like a heat seeking missile, Ryan flies through The Institute. Dodging corners and medical carts like he's been here a thousand times. The wall made of windows comes into view and he knows he's on the right path.

A group of people are standing in the hallway. A small lady in a white coat had her back to him. He's getting close to his target.

It takes all of his strength to be as polite as possible. "Excuse me. I would like to see my daughter, please?"

The lady in the white coat turns toward him and he recognizes her from the other day. That's the lady who gagged Rachel. "Is your daughter being released today? I wasn't aware of any discharges."

"No, I don't think so. My wife and I never got a phone call, but we would like to see our daughter and take her home." Ryan can feel his blood pressure rising.

"Im sorry, sir. None of our patients are going home today. We don't know what's happening to them and we don't have a cure yet."

"That's fine. I'll bring her back when you do have a cure. You're not keeping my baby here. How do you even know she has this disease? It could just be the flu or some shit."

"Sir, your daughter has been bitten. She's already starting to change. We have to keep her here."

"Wh-what do you mean she's been bitten? When was she bitten? She didn't tell us she was bitten." Ryan's blood pressure soars even higher.

"She has a bite mark on her shoulder that's infected. We examined her when you brought her here. She didn't tell you? You didn't see it?"

"No." Laura's voice is quiet and shaky from behind Ryan.

"No. She didn't tell us." Ryan tells the doctor. He feels as if his soul has just left his body. He feels empty inside.

"Well, once you've been bitten it's guaranteed you will turn into whatever those things are." The doctor says. "Your daughter is turning. We can't let her leave."

"Like hell you can. Take me to my daughter now."

"Sir, that's not a good-"

"TAKE ME TO MY DAUGHTER NOW!!" Ryan's blood pressure finally boils over. He's one step away from tearing this place apart brick by fucking brick.

The doctor nods her head. "Okay, sir. Please follow me."

# Ryan/Laura

## A New Rachel

# Chapter 25

T he elevator felt like it was hardly moving. Ryan felt like he was about to explode. He was never very patient. The news of his daughter being bitten took the air right out of his lungs. He had no idea. Rachel kept it a secret. Why did she do that?

Bile starts to rise from his stomach and into his throat. Ryan's whole body feels numb. What were they walking into?

The elevator doors open and the doctor walks out first. Ryan feels like he can't move but the adrenaline propels him forward. He follows the doctor with Laura right behind him. The first room they see has a boy in it with rust colored hair. His eyes are glazed over and blood is covering his snarling teeth. His movements are twitchy and erratic. Laura gasps and covers her mouth. Tears start to run down her face.

At the end of the hall there's a room with another kid in it. A girl with long brown hair. She slowly lifts her head up and looks like she starts to sniff the air. She makes eye contact with them as they walk up to her room.

It's Rachel.

Laura lets out a wail as she falls to her knees.

"Give. Me. My. Daughter. Now." Ryan says stern but calm.

The doctor pulls out a key card and unlocks Rachel's door. Before pushing the door fully open she says to Ryan, "Sir, I am highly against this. She could-"

Ryan puts his hand up, stopping her. All he wants is his daughter. No one and he means no one will get in his way. He rushes to Rachel's side. He moves her hair away from her face as a low growl comes out of her mouth. She smells horrible. Like rotten meat. Maybe all she needs is a nice warm shower and some over the counter medicine. It might not work, but by god he is going to try anything to save his daughter.

He scoops her up in his arms and carries her out of the room. He located his target. Now it's time to get her home.

******

Ryan and Laura are nervous wrecks driving home. The girl in the back seat is not their daughter. Her body twitches and jerks around uncontrollably. Her once joyful smile is now a horrible snarl. Her bright eyes are now dark and sad; there's nothing behind them.

A low, ominous growl comes out of her every so often. Rachel has never made that sound before. Is she really turning into an animal?

Laura wonders if this disease resembles rabies. The aggression, fever, fatigue. It would make sense. Once you show symptoms of rabies it is almost always fatal. The only way to test for rabies is a brain sample. Laura hopes they're doing the right thing.

Back at home, Laura and Ryan get Rachel inside. The bodies littering the sidewalk serve as a dark reality if Rachel doesn't get better.

Inside their home, Ryan sits Rachel down at the kitchen island. "How about some lunch, honey? You must be hungry. I know hospital food sucks." Laura says trying to be as cheerful as possible.

"Lunch sounds great to me." Ryan says. "I'm starving. I'll be right back. I gotta use the john." Before leaving Ryan gives Rachel a kiss on her head.

Laura starts to pull stuff from the fridge to make sandwiches. She hears the chair scrap across the floor. She turns around to find Rachel standing right next to her. "Honey, are you okay?"

Rachel growls and grabs her mom by the arm—slamming her teeth into her skin. Laura screams and falls backwards. Rachel clamps down harder, tearing and pulling off a chunk of flesh. Immediately, Rachel goes for her mom's throat. Her teeth slicing and snapping the jugular vein.

Ryan runs back into the room still zipping up his pants. "What was that? What's-" Ryan sees Rachel on the floor bent over. He hears tearing and squelching. Rachel stops eating to face the smell of another meal.

Ryan can't believe what he's seeing. Is that Laura? She isn't moving or saying anything. Is she...dead? Rachel starts to stumble towards her dad. Snarling and growling with fresh blood and flesh stuck to her face.

Ryan can only think of one thing to do. Rachel isn't Rachel anymore. He has to do the right thing. Just like

Matt had to do. He runs up to his room and gets his small handgun from under the bed. A Smith and Wesson.

He slowly makes his way back downstairs. Shuttering at any noise he hears coming from Rachel. He hears her shuffling around. He comes around the corner and sees Rachel in the archway of the kitchen. He raises his gun. "I'm sorry, baby." He whispers to Rachel as tears roll down his face.

A *pop* echoes through the house.

Ryan roars as his body collapses. His wife and his daughter are both dead. The silence in the house was heavy, suffocating.

He always promised he could never live without them.

He raises his gun and points it at his head.

*Pop.*

# Police Chief
# Bahrke

# Epilogue

Six feet is the standard depth for a grave.  Matt could only dig about three. The ground was still hard from the freezing night before—at least that's what he told himself. In reality, the big guy had a mental breakdown while burying his wife and youngest son. He was glad no one was around to see.

He wanted the kids to see him as unstoppable. Strong. Unbreakable. They already saw him cry once.

He was still human after all—for now.

Matt finishes the grueling task and prays for his family. He says his last goodbyes and leaves his old world behind.

He sees the faces of his family in all of the bodies still covering the street. He wonders what will be done with them. He'll move them if he has to—so the faces will go away.

What about inside all of the houses? There must be more bodies he thinks as he looks around the quiet, deserted street. The thought of going house to house playing plague doctor already has him exhausted.

First things first, he has some hungry teenagers to take care of.

Back at Zoe's house the kids were just starting to stir. Zoe half expected her mom to be asleep next to her on the couch—drunk. When there was no sign of her, Zoe had a sickening feeling that something was wrong. She reaches for her phone only to find she has no service. She wonders what could have happened to her.

Chief Bahrke enters the house covered in sweat and dirt. "Oh, good. I'm glad you guys are waking up. I need to talk to everyone."

The boys wipe the sleep out of their eyes and sit up from their sleeping spots. The chief stands in front of them as if he was doing roll call. "I know you guys have been through a lot these past couple of days, but I think it's time we think about our survival."

"Survival?" Zoe questions.

The chief nods. "In our training, we are taught that movement means life. You never stay in one spot for too long. We're already low on food and it may take time for anyone to help us."

"What about my mom?" Zoe asks.

"We can look for her on our way and you can leave her a note, okay?"

"We'll have to get my parents too." Taylor replies.

"Don't forget about Rachel." Elijah answers.

"We'll grab Rachel and Taylor's parents too. This might be our only chance to leave."

The kids agree without any arguments. They trust the chief. He's also the only adult around. They grab whatever non-perishable food they can find, which isn't much.

As Zoe writes a note for her mom, two *pops* of gunfire startle the group. Matt reaches for his 9mm on instinct. It sounded close. Too close.

Matt gets the kids piled into his car and tells them he'll go check on Rachel and her family. He approaches their house and knocks on their door. "Ryan? Laura? It's Matt. Can I talk to you?" Their car is in their driveway. He knocks a couple more times with no answer. He decides to check the house out.

The front door opens without a problem and he can see right away that Ryan is lying in a pool of blood with a gun next to him. He can see Rachel. She's not moving. Another figure is lying in the kitchen. It must be Laura. There were only two gunshots.

Matt slowly and carefully enters the house. Ryan has a hole in his head. Self inflicted Matt assumes. Rachel has been shot in the head as well. She doesn't look like Rachel anymore. He bends down to check Laura's pulse. She's gone. No gunshot, but she's been bitten.

He exits the house and slowly closes the door.

Back at his car, he gets into the driver's seat. "Is Rachel coming?" Taylor asks.

The chief hesitates. "No. No, they're not coming right now." The chief lies in order to protect them. He starts the engine and starts driving towards Taylor's house. He prays silently to himself, hoping for a better outcome—hoping Taylor's parents are alive.

TO BE CONTINUED...

# Acknowledgements

To the reader,

Thank you for reading my debut novel! I would love to hear your feedback about my book. If you liked it, hated it or anything in between. Your input can make me a better writer in the future. I plan to write more stories so keep a look out!

Send me your thoughts at brooke_lutherbooks@yahoo.com